For my own little cub, Jay, with love
M.M.

This edition published by Parragon Books Ltd in 2013 and distributed by

Parragon Inc.
440 Park Avenue South, 13th Floor
New York, NY 10016
www.parragon.com

Published by arrangement with Gullane Children's Books
Text and Illustrations: © Mark Marshall 2008

ISBN 978-1-4723-3188-5

Printed in China

Little Leopard
on the Move

Mark Marshall

Bath · New York · Singapore · Hong Kong · Cologne · Delhi
Melbourne · Amsterdam · Johannesburg · Shenzhen

Little Leopard was happy.
Every day, he played with his
friends and snoozed in the shade.
Life couldn't be better.

But one day, his mommy had some news.
"Little Leopard," she said, "now that you are getting
bigger, we will have to find a home with more space."

"I don't want a new home!" squeaked
Little Leopard. "I like it here,
near all my friends!"

Little Leopard ran away to find Elephant.

"Hello, Little Leopard," smiled
Elephant, "what's with the sad face?"
"Mommy says now that I'm getting bigger, we
need a new home," sighed Little Leopard.
"But if we move, I'll miss you!"

"Then why don't you come and live with me?" said Elephant.
"We can splish and splash in the water all day long."

But the water was too cold and wet for
Little Leopard, so he ran off to find the Meerkats.

"Hello, Little Leopard,
what's with the sad face?" asked the Meerkats.
"Mommy says now that I'm getting bigger, we need a new home,"
sighed Little Leopard. "But if we move, I'll miss you!"

"Then why don't you come and live with us?"
said the Meerkats. "We can race and dive into
our sandy burrows all day long."

But the burrows were too small and dark for Little Leopard, so he scampered off to find Zebra.

"Hello, Little Leopard,
what's with the sad face?" asked Zebra.
"Mommy says now that I'm getting bigger, we need a new home,"
sighed Little Leopard. "But if we move, I'll miss you!"

"Then why don't you come and live with me?" cried Zebra.
"We can play hide-and-seek in the tall grass all day long!"

But the grass was too tickly and scratchy for
Little Leopard, so he ran off to find the Lizards.

"Hello, Little Leopard, what's with the sad face?" asked the Lizards.
"Mommy says now that I'm getting bigger, we need a new home,"
sighed Little Leopard. "But if we move, I'll miss you!"

"Then why don't you come and live with us?"
cried the Lizards. "We can sunbathe
on the rocks all day long!"

But the rocks were too hard,
and the sun was too hot
for Little Leopard.

Sadly, Little Leopard made his way back to his mommy.

"What's with the sad face, little one?" she asked.

"I don't want to move!" sobbed Little Leopard. "I'll miss my friends."

"Silly thing!" smiled Mommy. "Come with me!"

Little Leopard followed
his mommy through the jungle.
High in the hills was a huge tree with
lots of leaves and branches.
"This is our new home!" said Mommy.

"Wow!" cried
Little Leopard
excitedly, racing
up the tree . . . .

"I get my very own branch, and
I can still see all my friends!

Goodnight, everyone!"